DARK NIGHT BRIGHT DAY

AN EYEWITNESS REPORT OF THE DIEM COUP IN SAIGON, VIETNAM 1-2 NOVEMBER 1963

by

CHRISTOPHER KING 1ST LT USAF
(WRITTEN 2-4 NOVEMBER 1963)

Cover Photo: C. King, *Mekong River in Soc Trang, 1963*

Blue Logic Publication
http://bluelogic.us
All rights reserved © 2013
by
Christopher King

ISBN 978-0-9835253-2-5

CHRISTOPHER KING 1ST LT USAF 1963

INTRODUCTION

I came to Vietnam as a first lieutenant in the United States Air Force in the summer of 1963—July I think—for a 14-month tour of duty. Only a few months after my arrival, the events described below took place, followed in a few weeks by the assassination of President Kennedy on November 22nd.

Shortly before I left Vietnam and the U.S. Air Force for good, the Gulf of Tonkin incident took place in early August of 1964, and led eventually to a massive build-up of American troops. During my period, however, there were fewer than 20,000 of us there.

In this brief introduction, I will not attempt to give either a public history of the Vietnam War, or a private history of my time there, but only some context and a little flavor of my life at the time. I was stationed near the city of Soc Trang (the Cambodian name) or Khanh

Christopher climbing into jet trainer

Hung (the Vietnamese name) in the far south of Vietnam in the Mekong River delta. I was at a joint Air Force and Army base, and the army troops had the nickname of the Soc Trang Tigers, since they had had a pet tiger until a few months before my arrival. I furnished the Air Force with an 11-foot boa constrictor, bought on the black market for $23, and later donated to the Army, but we never became known as the Soc Trang Snakes!

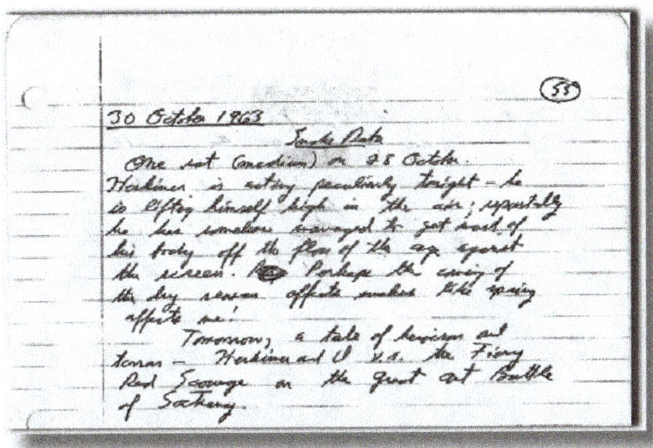

My official role was intelligence. Unfortunately, almost all of my intelligence was useless because of a fluid, rapidly shifting military situation; I rarely got intelligence even as fresh as one day old. My unofficial role included entertaining visiting brass, including a four-star admiral, with my snake. It also involved rounding up in a truck

Lt. King and boa constrictor

what we called our 'sacrificial lambs'—
Vietnamese Air Force troops, mostly kids who
knew nothing about flying—to accompany our
pilots on their missions in T-28's, old propeller-
powered double-seated trainers. We were
'advisors', so by some strange logic we had to
have Vietnamese, qualified or not, flying along
with our pilots in the back seat.

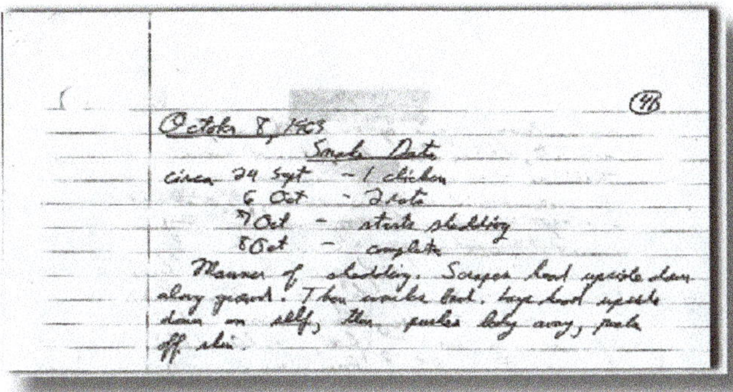

Lt. King and friends

The great snake news of recent days is that Herkimer
[i]ot a he nor a python. The Vietnamese beterinarian that
Marero brought for me was quite definite about the
[...]a male has testicles, this snake did not, ergo it is
[...]le (although this doesn't rule out castrated males).

T-28's ready to take off

T-28 taxis down runway

Vietnamese lady

I, like many others, had Vietnamese girlfriends, and learned the sardonic phrase that one leaves one's loved ones and goes back to one's dependents when departing from Vietnam. I also learned that at the same time we were trying to 'win the hearts and minds' of the Vietnamese, a phrase often repeated, many of my fellow Americans were calling them 'gooks'.

I got myself back, and wisted impatienlty for many more
minu es. McKinney and Walker returned from a prty their
landlady had thrown, in high"spirits" and seeing me there
began to laugh and then promised to inquire at the bar
once more. But, as it turned out, they were more interestd
ingetting themselves a couple of young ladies. No matter,
for just before they returned with their charming mademoiselles,
Ann finally appeared.

Narrative continued. Significant events of today--
none. Routine, quite routine. "War" is hardly hell here.
It is rather meaning less to many of the men here I am
afraid, especially those whose direct role in supporint
our combat planes is slight.

I ought to be coable of at least one good thought
before I close. I though one earlier today, but I'll be
damned if I can remember it. Worthy of a philosopher, it
was. Some general concept, none of your gross immediates
if you please.

26 December 1963

Tonight I will describe as well as I can remeber my
last tryst with Ann. I was not able to bed her during the
time of the coup due to the damnably early curfew. Returning to Saigon about the tenth of November, via a trip
to Bien Hoa to coordinate intelligence matters which it
turned out no longer needed to be coordinated because I was
no longer attached to them, I successfully persuaded her
to come to the domicile of McKinney and Walker. I had the
whole lower floor to myself. After paying the usual 1600
piastres it costs to release her from her duties, I departed
and impatiently waited for minute after minute. Finally,
losing my patience, I left a note on the door and returned
to the bar where I was vehemently assured by her friends
that she had indeed left and that I had better get back if
I didn't want to miss her.

I remember many things, among them, the mortaring of our base twice, and the deaths of several of my pilot friends. More vividly than anything else except the coup, I remember being asked by one of my Army pilot friends to throw a low-ranking Vietnamese officer out of a helicopter. I had gone along for a ride in one of

Huey helicopter at Soc Trang

two Army helicopters on a visit to a Special Forces camp in a coastal mangrove swamp. The other helicopter had been damaged by enemy fire, and we could only allow a certain number of people to board our helicopter if we were to be able to take off. I could not do it when I saw the terrified look in his eyes. My friend left his cockpit seat and did it for me, but never said a word about it. (I should add that the helicopter was on the ground at the time!)

What I remember best of all, though, happened in early November, 1963. I and three friends were staying in a hotel near the presidential palace during the night of the 1st and the early morning of the 2nd, and the words which follow this introduction were written in the dark with a pencil and whatever paper I could find as I watched a small portion of the events that overthrew and destroyed Ngo Dinh Diem, the then President of Vietnam. What I experienced after leaving the hotel in the morning was written down within a day or two. Later I typed much of what I had written, and then nearly forgot about it for more than forty-five years, until I showed it to my friend Gilbert Moore one day, and his enthusiastic reception led to this tiny book. I hope that the words which you will find below, now nearly fifty years old, will bring you some small idea of what it was like then.

Christopher King   Oregon House, CA
21 September 2011

An oncoming boa constrictor

NIGHT

The time is 3:30 AM Saturday morning, November 2, 1963. Place: a third story balcony two blocks east of the Gia Long palace, Saigon. This is the site of the last great battle of the coup which started more than fourteen hours ago on Friday afternoon with simultaneous attacks all over the city. All the other strong points have fallen, and now Diem is making his last stand in his heavily defended palace fortress.

Here I sit on Le Thanh Ton Street listening to mortar shells whizzing back and forth overhead. From our grandstand seat four of us have been watching most of the night through—it's no time to be sleeping. Over our heads we can hear the eerie high-pitched gradually descending whistle of the incoming and outgoing mortar shells, followed by huge crashes, now in the distance, now close at hand. Far off we can hear the lazy drone of airplanes and we wonder if a bombing is near. The full moon is out, but a haze adds a ghostly tinge to the entire spectacle.

Now it's about 3:45 in the morning and this has been going on about half an hour. You hear a high-pitched gradually descending (but very little) whistle-whizzing, a moment of silence, and then the impact. They seem to be whizzing back and forth just above our trees, but this may

Here I sit on a second storey balcony of a house
on [illegible] street in Saigon listening to what
that is [illegible] shells [illegible] back and forth over
head. It's about 3:45 in the morning and the [illegible]
been going on for [illegible] about ½ hour. You hear a
high-pitched, gradually descending (but very little) chuckle, which
a [illegible] of [illegible] and the [illegible] expect. They
seem to be [illegible] back just above our heads, but
[illegible]

For the past 20 minutes [illegible]
[illegible]

Wait, [illegible] down [illegible] to the left;
now the [illegible] flare is rising. It's 4:00
now, 4:a [illegible] the [illegible] of [illegible]
The [illegible]

(Notes scribbled in dark at 2 November 1943)

be an illusion. Next door an unanswered phone has been ringing for what seems like hours. Now there is a movement of armored cars down the street to our left, blocking it off.

For the past twenty minutes planes—it sounds like a couple of T-28's—have been circling the area, but nothing has opened up on them yet. There is a full moon out, but visibility is limited by a haze.

For a while now under a hazy full moon everything has quieted down, so I'll take the opportunity to recapitulate the day so far.

Wait, some shots down the street to the left; now the mortar fire is resuming. It is 4:00 now, 4:00 in the afternoon of Friday back home. Pro-regime troops just down the street from us around Diem's place of residence.

A few minutes of silence are rudely interrupted by tremendous explosions only two blocks down the street to our left, just in front of the south wall of the palace. And now the heavy barking of the .50 caliber machine guns and the lighter staccato chatter of the .30's has begun.

The main attack has begun from the south on the heels of a diversionary attack a half hour earlier from the north. Now a tank squeaks and clanks its way down our street and stops almost directly in front of our balcony. There it sat the rest of the night, its muzzle pointing eastward to ward off an attack that never came. I did not see it, but [a] fellow witness says it was soon abandoned, though a radio in it kept playing; we saw later in the morning light that it had caught on a barbed wire barricade. He's just sitting out front idling his engine. Engine makes an odd sort of chirping noise. Always in the background automatic fire, rifle shots, and a few booms. [*Badly garbled passage.*] (The chirping noise turned out to be something other than the tank, for I heard it the next day. Probably associated with some electric equipment) . . . while I gaze out the third floor balcony down on roads(?) and trees. Now renewal of weapons fire with a few thunderclaps, but all in the distance.

Bursts of attacking weapons fire now, the flash of incoming mortars and return weapons fire clearly visible, terrifyingly audible. Shouts of men. Some of the mortar rounds being . . .

Can't remember when it left off, but tinkles on the roof from some of the mortars' pieces. Heavy automatic fire .30 and .50 caliber just down the street. Short while ago building and defenders just down the street lit in lurid pink glow. Mortars landing just one block away. (Was actually two blocks away, by palace.) Loud, frequent, long automatic weapons fire, punctuated by silences.

For more than two hours the symphony of the guns rages at irregular intervals, with long moments of silence suddenly interrupted by terrific rampaging bursts. The long red floating lances of tracer fire flash in all directions. Suddenly there is a huge yellow flare of light, a gigantic concussion, and three swiftly following lesser blasts. A tank blowing up near the palace. For several minutes we can hear its ammunition bursting and crackling like popcorn in some infernal skillet.

Now weapons being cocked below us. Booming more frequent now. Weapons fire louder. All quiet for a short while. There's a .50 down the street and around the corner cutting loose. Now from across the way peaceful chirping. Incongruously. About 4:50. At 4:00 most of the lights went out. Up till that time the whole city had remained well-lit.

Bursts of gunfire, a thunderclap, tinkling fragments and the silence punctuated only by the tank's chirping, which I've been told is the fan belt.

Just who cut the lights off or why is as yet unknown.

The tank out front presumably belongs to the presidential brigade and armored elite who are guarding the president well tonight. Now the damn phone's ringing again.

A couple of thunderclaps, and more rampaging bursts of .30 caliber then—silence and chirping. The whole battle so far seems to

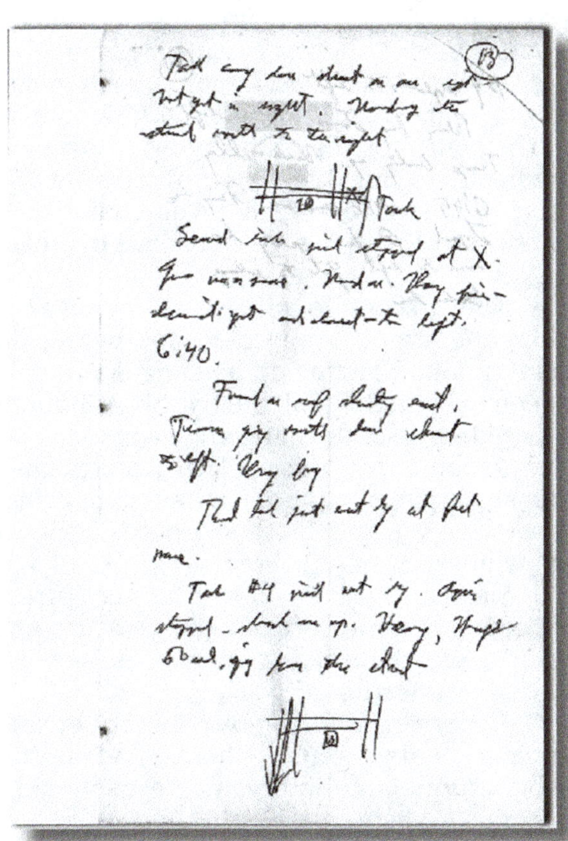

have been mostly east-west, but it's hard to say from my vantage (or was it disadvantage? [*Added later*]) point. Continuous fire now. Silence—sporadic bursts. Soon the dawn will come.

Now there's fire visible going north coming from our rear. Must be the good guys coming from the south for Diem's bad guys. Heavy fire immediately to our rear. More tracers—a very nearby thunderclap—much tinkling of debris. Down the street and left, yellow points of muzzle flash.

Now tracer fire going east. Whose? A voice in the street. The quiet tank below, the brilliant moon reflecting off a nearly dry puddle. Between me and the tank the twisting silhouette of a large tree—somewhat comforting.

A moment of silence. Then it starts again. Rampaging bursts. (And I mean rampaging.) [*Added later.*] Tracer fire going north again. A bullet whines across the street.

Silence again. Voice in the street, questionings. Some sort of night creature now making a weird throaty two-level noise. His voice rudely interrupted.

Tracer going north now. Pattern of sorts emerging. Violent bursts, then silence. With mortars at indefinite intervals. Certainly not a continuous firefight.

Now flames are visible down the street to our left. Looks like a burning building—could

be a tree. Phone still ringing. Time now 5:00.
More tracers, going north. Lots of them.

Tank chirping has stopped.

A few ominous bolt clicks. Now tracer going southeast.

Now silence again, always silence.

A .50 cutting away at a great rate down the street. A war of sounds—one can see so little. Another slug just tranged past. I suppose there's a little risk out here on the balcony, but not enough to withdraw.

Damn mosquitoes ever faithful. War in the midst of war.

Several [*Illegible words*] going down the street. Voices and noise as of many men down and left. Where ignorant armies clash by night. Several people running east down our street away from the palace.

Two blasts—our hotel shakes. Two cracks of rifle right outside.

Some shots right down our street—rifle. Can easily see muzzle flash.

The symphony of guns rages all around us. There are the deep bass explosions of the mortar, the fierce heavy surging of the heavy caliber weapons, the rattle of the lighter caliber, and finally a few pop-gun pops right outside.

(Some of the so-called mortar rounds were tanks firing recoilless 57mm rifles and 75mm guns.) [*Added later.*]

This damn tank out front is useless.

I can see the .50 caliber thundering down the street, but can't tell what direction he's shooting in.

The damn phone is still ringing.

Time flies—5:45 already.

MORNING

Our .50 caliber going at a great rate, off and on, for the past five minutes. A parachute flare to the south lighting things up with a green glow for 10-15 seconds. Tracer fire going east over our heads. Fierce firefight seeming to come from palace grounds. Dying down for a while.

Starting up again.

Right next to us on the balcony stands a big red national (?) sign: Royal Air Lao.

Our .50 caliber [?] firing south. All of a sudden tremendous flash right by it. Yellow flare-up, glowing. No more fire from him. (Turned out to be a tank blowing up.) Apparently his ammo was hit. Bursts of it are going off at random. Three secondary blasts—random ammo shells going off—sounding like popcorn in a popper.

Explosion coming from out left again— hard to tell if ammo blowing up or mortar dropping in. Three explosions in a row from .50 caliber direction—clearly not mortar. Ammo going off in burst after burst. Ammo going off sporadically sounds something like a giant chewing lettuce.

Suddenly across the street . . . .

Tremendous yellow burst from the .50 caliber. Ammo going up, mortar blast, or both.

Not much silence now.   Tremendous

heavy burst from left—two .50's? Slug whizzes by, ends on roof above us. Two sharp cracks out front—can't sight shooter. Makes me nervous.

Tracer fire [*Illegible word*] going east. Perhaps from rooftop position I noticed earlier on in the afternoon. Tracer fire going south overhead. Tracer fire [*Illegible word*] a number of sharp cracks—we've got him located. On the roof across the street and to our left.

I am guessing that the palace is being attacked from north and south. Our tank still sits out here facing east, doing nothing.

Firefight to our left waxes and wanes in intensity. 6:20 now. It can't remain dark much longer.

The night animal is going again—sounds like a skipped needle on a rusty record spinning around the last end grooves.

Phone ringing across the way now. It's beginning to get light at an accelerated rate.

Dawn coming on fast.

Tremendous blast ½ block away. Hitting the corner. Much louder automatic fire stepping up, much nearer and louder, never a lull.

.50 caliber tracers going right down south on the street half a block to our left. [*Illegible word*] (Actually going down the street running by the palace. [Added later])

The evening is fading fast and the dawn is coming on with a rush. It can't last much longer now. All of a sudden four tanks go whining and clattering down the street a half block to our right at one minute intervals, and only a few moments later the heaviest firing yet breaks out, huge waves of terrifying sound that seem to fill the whole of Saigon.

Second tank just stopped. Moved on. Heavy fire nearest yet and closest to left. 6:40. Friend on roof shooting east.

Tracer going north down street to left. Very busy. *[?]*

Third tank just went by at fast pace.

Tank #4 just went by. Again stopped— shook me up. Heavy, heavy .50 caliber going down the street. Big explosions to left. (Probably tanks blowing hole through wall. [*Added later*])

A series of huge explosions. And suddenly silence. Now we can hear ragged shouts, which soon swell into continuous yelling and cheering. A whistle shrills again and again. It's all over! The palace has fallen at 6:40 Saturday morning, only a little more than three hours after the final onslaught began.

Palace being stormed to our left. Troops rushing up. Much yelling. Whistle shrilling again and again. 6:45. All seems over. Firing has stopped. Continuous yelling down road to left. Gate to palace broken down reports fellow watcher.

Immediately   after   this,   we   hastily

dressed (for me shoes with no socks) and left the building, first keeping cautiously behind trees, building corners, and lamp posts, then growing bolder. In a little while we decide to cross the cement area at the top of the park, and edge around the corner of the last building fronting along the street the Rex Hotel fronts on.

Suddenly striding down the street come two confident soldiers, guns carelessly held, heading straight for 'our' tank. (They soon 'captured' it.) They are so friendly -- though preoccupied with 'capturing' our tank, greeting us in English and when we asked "Finit?" replying "Finit!" -- that we fling caution to the winds and walk boldly down the street till we reach the corner of the massive palace wall.

INTO THE PALACE

In the southeast corner of the heavy brick wall there was a gaping hole about three feet in diameter, and about 2 or 3 feet off the sidewalk. Through this hole a line of soldiers was pouring, loaded down with weapons. We joined them in line, I boosted through a soldier with a particularly heavy weapon who had been boosting several of his comrades, and then was boosted through myself with my friend Ron McKinney on my heels. We paused in the corner of the palace gardens looking at the battered hulk of the palace, while soldiers in olive drab rushed past us like ants. We thought we'd done

pretty well, but even so, there were a few other Americans ahead of us, mostly correspondents and photographers.

After we are sure there will be no more shooting, we enter the spacious rooms of the first floor. The palace has suffered surprisingly little, considering the scale and intensity of the battle which was raging around it such a short time ago. Outside, except for a few large holes, most of the damage seems to be innumerable pockmarks blasted by bullets, gaps where chunks of cornice are missing, and shattered windows and dangling shutters. Inside, fallen plaster and broken glass, overturned furniture, scuffed-up rugs, and dozens of metal ammunition cases give mute testimony to the intensity of the recent struggle. But strangely enough this litter seems almost lost in the huge high-ceilinged room; in one room long rows of tables and chairs stand perpendicular to a huge mirrored mantel, all untouched by any turmoil.

Soon after entering we ascend the grand staircase from the cavernous first floor rooms to the smaller and more livable rooms upstairs. Everywhere there are soldiers, enjoying their moment of triumph and looting to their heart's content. Their attitude towards us is surprising; the majority do not even seem aware of our presence, while those who do notice us go out of their way to be friendly, greeting us in their quaintly accented English.

There were no corpses in evidence; I learned later that the guard had surrendered, waving a white flag. Soon we joined the soldiers in the palace. It was a scene of describable [Intentional wording] confusion. Here in the stately, huge rooms where not so very long ago Mme. Nhu, husband, and brother-in-law had lived and moved, soldiers were rushing here and there or busily engaged in ransacking odd corners, drawers, back rooms. For the next half hour we wandered from room to room on both floors, frequently stopping to look at the various pieces of flotsam and jetsam the tide of the coup had turned our way.

The soldiers themselves were childlike, not only in their friendliness but also in their inability to understand many of the things which they discovered. Their ignorance of some of their discoveries is amusing. One brings me a bottle of French mouthwash, apparently thinking it is some sort of beverage. I soon give him to understand that it is 'number 10'—pidgin English for 'very bad'. One of my friends explains the fine art of lighting a cigar (first you bite off the end!) while another demonstrates a straight razor. One of the soldiers came to me with a box of candy, unopened, with a questioning look on his face as if to say "You're an American, you know about these things. Tell me what this is." So I opened it and gave him to understand the contents were most edible. Earlier, another soldier proudly and politely offered Ron and me our choice from an open box of candy which he held for us.

Everywhere in the upstairs rooms there seems to be a cloud of dust from the plaster shaken from the walls and ceiling by the heavy fighting. Through this haze the soldiers move rapidly to and fro, sorting through everything at hand in a hasty search for something of value, and creating an indescribable litter.

In the course of my wanderings upstairs, I come across what I know must be the Nhus' suite. Incongruous reminders of its former occupants are everywhere. Here is a built-in bookcase, all the upper shelves filled with album after album of photographs of the Nhus' public appearances; and there on a little round coffee table are pictures of a solemn little boy frolicking on some far-off seashore. A soldier brings me a set of records he has found in the suite. 'Deutsch Ohne Muhe' [*German without difficulty*] says the label. Later I gaze into the face of Ngo Dinh Nhu [*Diem's brother-in-law*] looking out from two mounted photographs in the bookcase; in one he wears military clothing, in the other the dress of a scholar.

The palace became progressively more untidy and fuller of soldiers. I began to cast around for some 'souvenir' to meditate on later in my life. I spent at least half my time in the palace browsing in what appeared to be Mme. Nhu's chambers, taking down several photograph albums, examining several gorgeously illustrated books, contemplating the pictures of Nhu as soldier and scholar, idly glancing through several pictures of the little boy romping on the seashore with assorted beachware, and engaging in small talk with the girl who writes for *Newsweek* (who incidentally was helping herself to some of Mme.'s extensive and expensive supply of perfumes, powders, soaps, etc.)

I started and stopped several times to abscond with one of the photo albums, but for some reason decided against it. (Perhaps I felt it was too personal a thing to take, although that is rather odd reasoning, because if you take something to remember a palace by, you would want it to be as 'intimate' as possible.)

Earlier, in another room, I had picked up an elegant ash tray. (It was in what appeared to be a planning room, for maps of South Vietnam were profuse.) Later, in the Nhu quarters I acquired a Paris tie. But my biggest piece of plunder came from downstairs in a vast room lined with conference tables and chairs. At its end, on the east wall of the palace, was a sort of mantel with a glass mirror for backing. On one side was a statue of a Cambodian dancer (which I later saw disappearing in the hands of an ARVN who gleefully admired and waved it); on the other was a large head of Buddha.

I picked it up and started to walk out, was warned against it by two other Americans, thought better and took it back, went back upstairs, was asked politely to leave by an ARVN [*Member of the Army of the Republic of Vietnam*] ("My captain not like") then resolved to wrap the head in a shirt and depart. So with a large white lump under my left arm, I departed.

The lack of bodies, as I said earlier, was due mostly to the fact that the palace guard had surrendered. Unfortunately, I did see one dead or dying man. He was lying on the south balcony on the second floor with his head toward the east, the upper part of his head covered by a blood-soaked blue cloth and framed by a large splotch of deep red blood. I know that he was still moving—his throat seemed to be working—but I am not sure that he was alive. Since I don't like to gape at such things I moved on and looked no more.

Later I learned that it was very doubtful indeed that he was alive for the whole back of his head had been blown away. A pathetic frail reminder that coups are not without their price.

But though the palace is filled with reminders of its former occupants, they are nowhere to be found; although Diem and Nhu were supposed to be in the palace when the final attack was launched, they have now fled. It is a relief to leave a place of endings and to walk the streets of Saigon as the city begins to whirl and jostle and babble and shout and honk and roar back to life after the long night of the coup.

ON THE STREET

Now that I look back I cannot but wonder and be thankful for the remarkable tolerance and friendliness of the ARVN soldiers. Here they had just finished a long grueling night of fighting, were invading the place for their reward, and along happen some upstart curious Americans. But they accepted us without question, as if we were one of them. Indeed several of them were especially friendly, greeting us first in our own tongue on several occasions. But most of them just accepted us as a normal and not-to-be-wondered-at part of the scene and left it at that. They were so terribly relieved.

In all that long period from Friday afternoon to Saturday morning I don't know of one American killed or even severely injured, a surprising fact considering that many of us managed to stick our noses in the most dangerous kinds of places. Another thing that is cause for wonder is the remarkable lack of damage visible in Saigon. With few exceptions, the damage was done only to buildings which were attack objectives. The exceptions that I know of were bookstores and printing offices, several of which were ransacked and burned. In some parts of Saigon, there were pages on the streets and sidewalks for scores of yards, enough reading for a lifetime underfoot.

After returning with my spoils and breakfasting, I set out once more to see what I could see. Soon being separated from my American companions, I stood in the middle of a dense Vietnamese crowd for nearly half an hour and watched the happy people of Saigon. Everywhere I looked I saw nothing but smiling faces, good spirits, admiration for the soldiers, and spontaneous bursts of laughter and applause. Americans seemed to be in excellent standing. I did not catch a single hostile look. Spontaneous parading.

Vietnamese kids in Soc Trang

After a while I caught the eye of a young ARVN sergeant, and for some reason looked again. He noticed, and before long he had gradually moved through the crowd and for several moments stood by my side, smiling at the antics of the people as was I. After a while we began talking, and Anh, as I shall call him from now on, proved to have a good vocabulary and a fair command of grammar. The rest of the day till 4:00 or 5:00 I spent in his company.

As I watched he explained to me some things which had puzzled me. For some time a white vehicle which I could not clearly see, since it was obscured by crowds of people, had been jolting back and forth through the crowd, noisily blowing a siren, and causing a good deal of merriment through the antics of its occupants. Anh explained that this vehicle had once belonged to President Diem. Anh also explained a series of announcements blaring from a nearby loudspeaker fastened to the cornice of a building opposite the southeast corner of the palace.

We had scrambled up the side of an armored personnel carrier (the whole intersection was filled with armored vehicles) and as the loudspeaker blared forth at each pause a huge cheer and loud clapping rose from the crowd; loaves of bread big and small were flying through the air almost as thick as the bullets that had flown earlier; sandwiches were brought by the hundreds and pressed on the soldiers and the bringers were enthusiastically cheered.

The loudspeaker was blaring forth . . . 'and so-and-so gives 500 piastres to the soldiers . . . so-and-so gives 1000 loaves of bread to the soldiers . . .'" and at each fresh announcement the cheers arose and the bread flew merrily at the appropriate time.

For several minutes during my breakfasting the air had been filled with shooting in celebration of the glorious events of November first and second, and now it started again. We scrambled down upon urgent orders from the vehicle driver and joined many other crowd members in their undignified rush to the shelter of nearby buildings. We, however, were more dignified, walking slowly to our haven. But no one was really very scared and everyone was grinning. Just some more happy soldiers.

Anh pointed out to me the major who had led the armored units which had led the coup. Scrambling up the armored vehicle again we gradually edged over to the next vehicle atop which Major Li Tung Ba stood surrounded by enthusiastic admirers. Anh hastened the process by voicing some low urgent remarks to each body which blocked our way, and they moved swiftly and unresentfully aside.

Finally I stood face to face with the major across a three foot gap. When we caught his attention, I saluted (which seemed to disturb Anh) and introduced myself. I asked him what plan he had used to attack. He explained that his first objective had been the presidential guard barracks which he attacked at twelve. (Visiting the place later in the afternoon on our way to the zoo—which was closed—Anh and I saw the signs of a fierce struggle. The gate bore the most marks of violence, but the entire four-block length was pockmarked.)

After his success there his next objective was the palace. His plan, which jibes with most of my combat observations, was to attack with his main force from the south with the bulk of his force at 4:00 after a diversionary attack from the north with a platoon at 3:30. He was not sure, said he, when he started that he would ever be able to capture such a strong point.

He was a fairly young man in his thirties, slim but well-knit, vital, handsome, and proud. Midway through our conversation we were interrupted by bursts of gunfire. The major immediately gave sharp strong orders for it to stop, and when it continued—because of the din—he became very wroth and summoned a subordinate who had his orders announced over the loudspeaker. Not realizing what he had decided, I suggested to him that he use the loudspeaker and was much embarrassed to learn he had already thought of that.

Soon after, our interview was concluded by me, and thanking the major, I carefully descended from my post. Anh was somewhat disgruntled with me in his gentle way because I had not remembered to ask what I said I was going to ask, namely, who were the masterminds behind the coup. I started back, but seeing that our major was once again engulfed and busy, we turned to another major and briefly asked him our question. I gathered that it was the high command collectively, and of course especially General Minh.

We journeyed on to the palace, stopping now and then to ask questions. I learned from a young ranger or paratrooper in camouflage clothing—who seemed quite flattered judging from his wide smile—that his unit had been nearby to keep order and shoot "high floor" (as Anh put it) snipers.

Arriving at the palace we strolled around to the north side, stood under a huge tree which seemed a twisted curtain of roots, and talked to another soldier who hadn't seen so much of the action. Everywhere we stopped to talk we collected a large circle of listeners.

The last 'coup event' was the most frightening. As we were moving along south on the west side of the palace, we suddenly heard the thunder of engines and in a second two T-28's appeared at rooftop level zooming towards the palace from the north. The crowd scattered on the instant, going anywhere to be out of the streets. We sprinted for an overhang on the corner of the palace wall and watched the others flee. One man was lifting his bicycle over the wall across the street. Soldiers in armored vehicles clicked their weapons, and pointing them upwards, looked grimly ready for fresh battle.

We moved quickly south away from the palace and finally came to a halt in the middle of the main street of Saigon and watched the T-28's make pass after pass. After several minutes I began to realize that they were only putting on an air show, and my fear quickly subsided. The whole time Anh had been saying "Do not be afraid, do not be afraid." His conduct touched me. Fearless, considerate, and sympathetic.

In the middle of the whole affair, which started about 11:15, while we were standing in the middle of the main street on a raised strip of concrete, another one of those spontaneous parades came toward us from down the street. Whether they regarded the planes as friend or foe I do not know, but I like to think those eager young faces were determined to do or die marching down the main street of their city waving their flag.

* * * * * * * * * * * * * *

Christopher King, 1ˢᵗ LT USAF
Saigon, Nov., 1963

APPENDIX A: ORIGINAL DIARY – SAIGON COUP – 11/03/1963

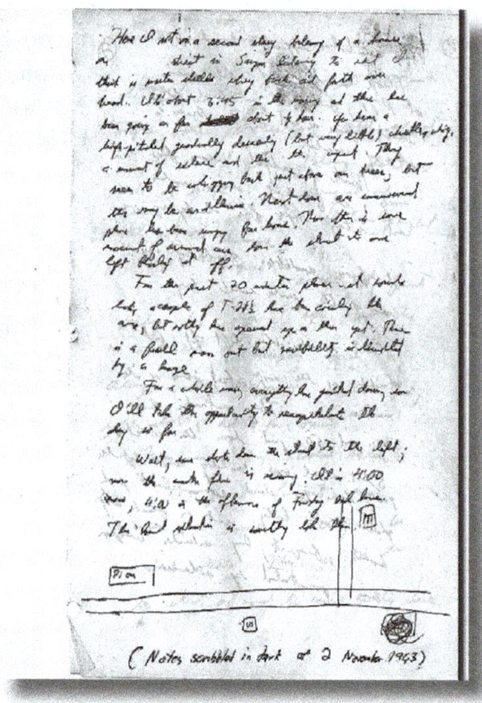

Troops ~~contributes support to forced~~ PTT

Troops cumulative of anti-aggression
at PTT, finally just saw it
silent from me and around their to
place of security.

Bouts of activity empire far
comes, & the flash of enemy article
and return wagon fire clearly visible,
terrifying audible. Shots of were
some of the under sounds being

Can't remember when left H, but
doubled on the roof from one of the
madam pre. Very automatic fire
30 and 50 just down the street.
S just which eye building and effected
just down the street act in level just
glow. Mature lady just in flash my
Loud, Bright, by automatic wagon
fire...punctuated by silence.

Here, from accounts very peaceful, strict [illegible], [illegible].

At 4:00 most of the lights went out.

My [illegible] told him the whole city had remained well [illegible].

Bursts of gunfire, a flickering glow, [illegible] frequently and then silence, punctuated [illegible] by the truth [illegible] sleeping, which I have been told is the [illegible].

Just why out the lights, my why is yet unknown.

The lights out front presumably [illegible] to the presidential brigade — an armored [illegible] [illegible] so quietly the president, well tonight. Here the loudspeaker [illegible] saying again.

A couple of flickering slaps, and now conveying [illegible] of [illegible], then — silence and [illegible] [illegible] [illegible] [illegible].

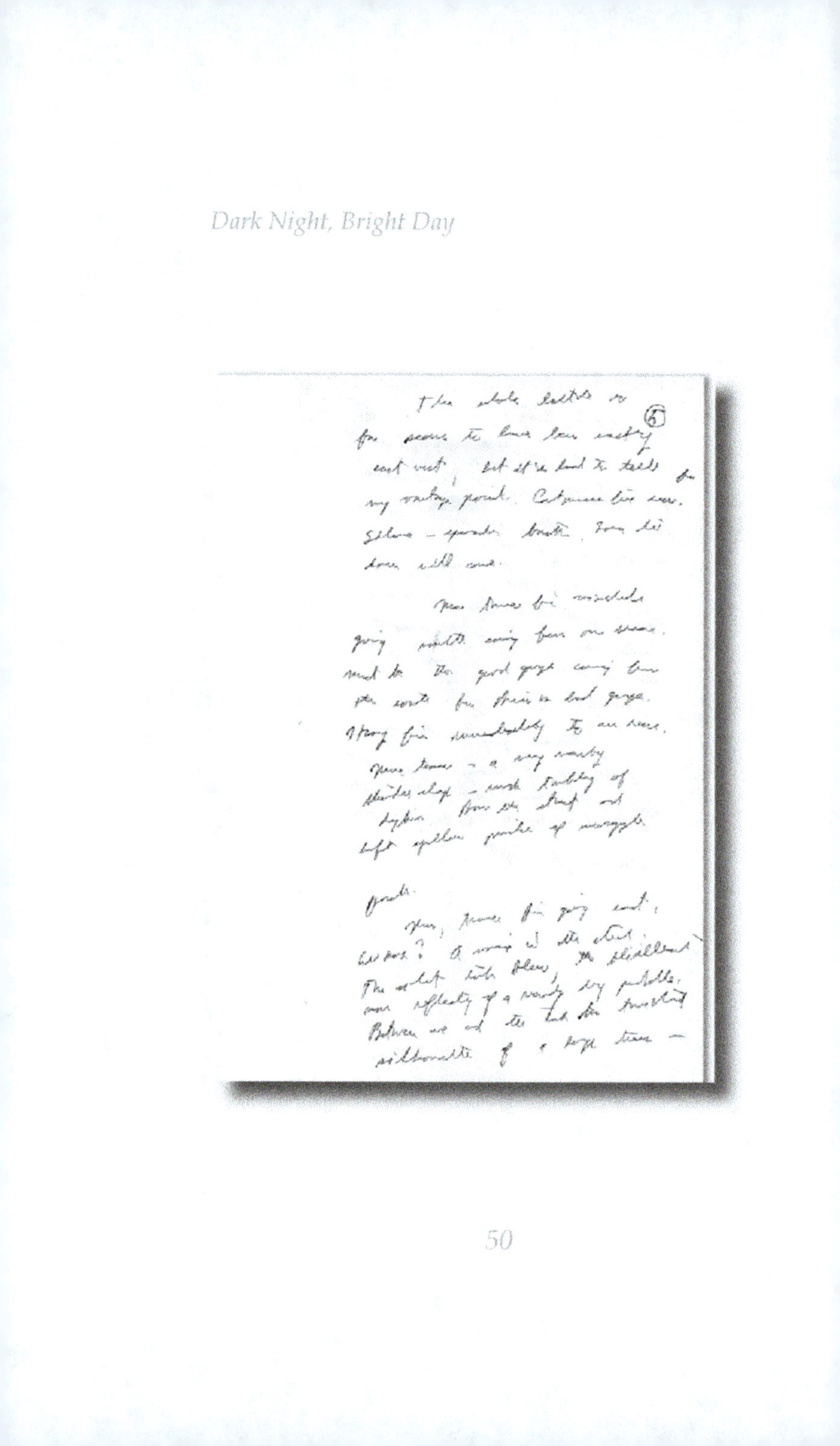

[illegible] [illegible] [illegible] ⑤
[illegible] [illegible] [illegible] [illegible]
[illegible] [illegible] [illegible] [illegible] [illegible]
[illegible] [illegible]. [illegible] [illegible] [illegible].
[illegible] — [illegible] [illegible], [illegible] [illegible]
[illegible] [illegible].

[illegible] [illegible] [illegible] [illegible]
[illegible] [illegible] [illegible] [illegible] [illegible].
[illegible] [illegible] [illegible] [illegible] [illegible] [illegible]
[illegible] [illegible] [illegible] [illegible] [illegible].
[illegible] [illegible] [illegible] [illegible] [illegible].
[illegible] [illegible] — [illegible] [illegible] [illegible]
[illegible] [illegible] — [illegible] [illegible] [illegible]
[illegible] [illegible] [illegible] [illegible]
[illegible] [illegible] [illegible] [illegible] [illegible]

[illegible].
[illegible], [illegible] [illegible] [illegible] [illegible],
[illegible]? [illegible] [illegible] [illegible] [illegible] [illegible]
[illegible] [illegible] [illegible] [illegible], [illegible] [illegible]
[illegible] [illegible] [illegible] [illegible] [illegible] [illegible].
[illegible] [illegible] [illegible] [illegible] [illegible] [illegible]
[illegible] [illegible] [illegible] [illegible] [illegible] —

[illegible] perfectly.

A moment's silence. Then it built
again. Tapping noise. [illegible] two
going work again. A cyclist [illegible]
crosses the street.

Silence again. Voices in the
street, questioning. [illegible] out of [illegible]
[illegible] only a [illegible] sharply
the [illegible] word. You were suddenly
interrupted.

Trace going [illegible] on.
Pattern of note emerging. Violent
[illegible] the silence. [illegible] entered at
[illegible] untoward. Certainly not
extraneous five-[illegible].

New planes are visible down the ⑤
street to our left. Looks like a burning
building — and be a tree. There
still saying. This now 5:00
[illegible] times, going [illegible]. Lots
of it
Tank driving by stopped
Soldiers [illegible] a shot — a painful
thing with fire.
A few minutes later chicken.
now tower going [illegible].
After silence gone, always silence.

Ct. 5:0 [illegible] my at
a great roll [illegible] to street. A row
of [illegible] — One can see so little.
[illegible] [illegible] just [illegible] past.
I suppose there's a little end at
here on the [illegible], but not enough
to withdraw.

Paw [illegible] am [illegible].
now in most of us.

Several [illegible] [illegible] going
down the street. [illegible] and [illegible]
[illegible] as of way are down at left

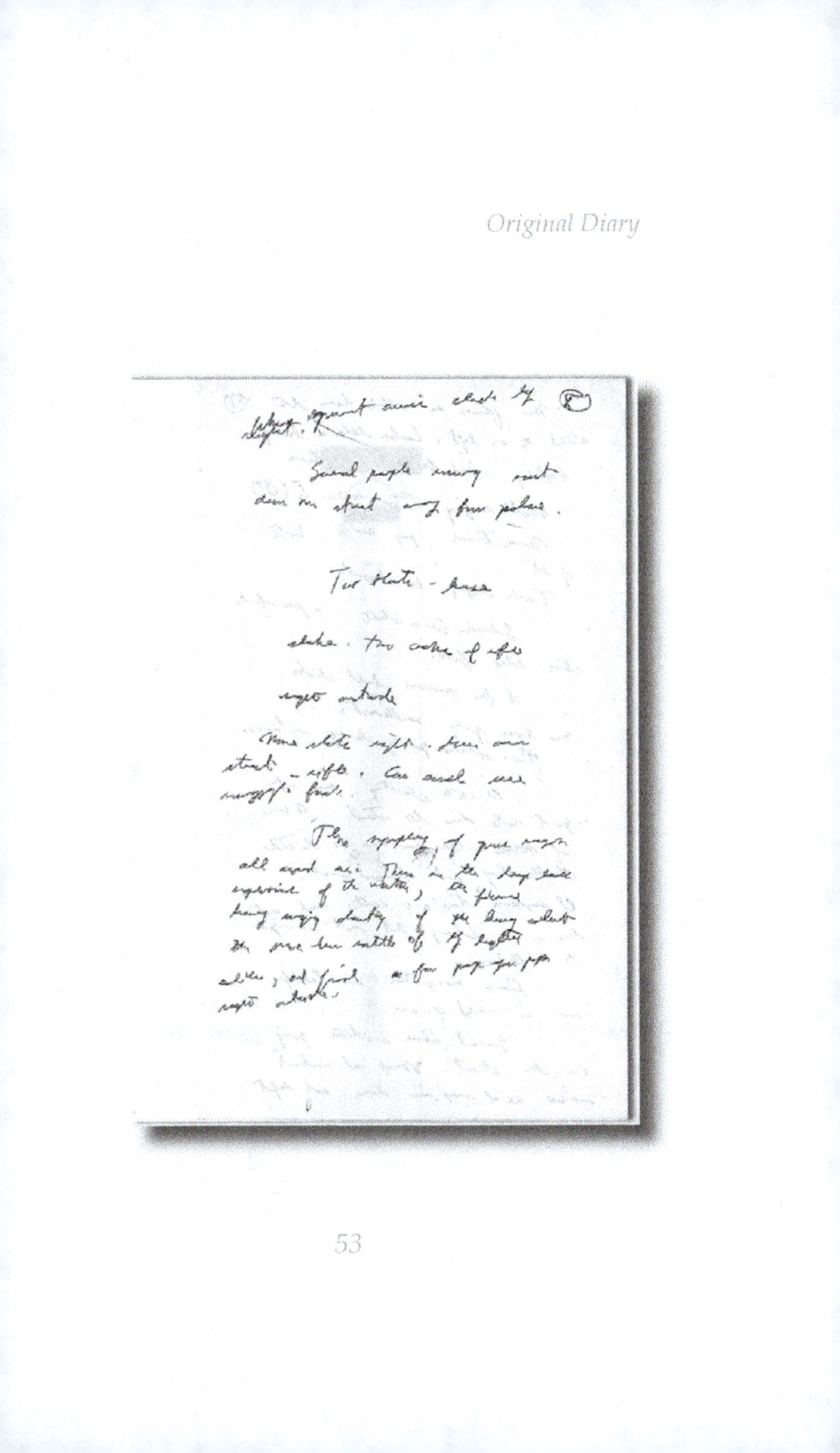

This [illegible] that object is useless

I can see the .50 caliber
[illegible] down the street, but can't tell
what direction hale standing in.
The alarm phone is still ringing.
This place — 5:45 already.

Then .50 [illegible] the [illegible]
[illegible] off and on, [illegible] the past five [illegible].
A [illegible] [illegible] to the north lighting
[illegible] up with a green fire [illegible]
60 — 15 [illegible]. Then fire going
out [illegible] on [illegible]. From the first
[illegible] the free [illegible] [illegible]
[illegible] may be a while
[illegible] my [illegible].
[illegible] out it on [illegible]
with a big red [illegible] sign
[illegible] air [illegible] low.

[illegible] [illegible] but [illegible]
50 [illegible]. [illegible] going up, [illegible]
[illegible], or both?

[illegible] above [illegible] [illegible]
[illegible] [illegible] on left — 2507 [illegible]
[illegible] of [illegible] above [illegible]
[illegible] sharp [illegible] out but — [illegible]
[illegible] [illegible]. [illegible] [illegible]

[illegible] bright [illegible] [illegible]
[illegible] from [illegible] [illegible] [illegible]
[illegible] [illegible] — in the [illegible]
[illegible] [illegible] [illegible] [illegible] [illegible].
[illegible] [illegible] [illegible] number of
[illegible] [illegible] — [illegible] not [illegible]
[illegible]. On the [illegible] [illegible]
[illegible] [illegible] [illegible] to my left.
I am [illegible] that the
[illegible] is by [illegible] [illegible]
[illegible] and [illegible]. On [illegible] [illegible]
[illegible] out [illegible] [illegible], [illegible].
[illegible] [illegible] on left [illegible]
at [illegible] is [illegible] 6:30

[illegible]

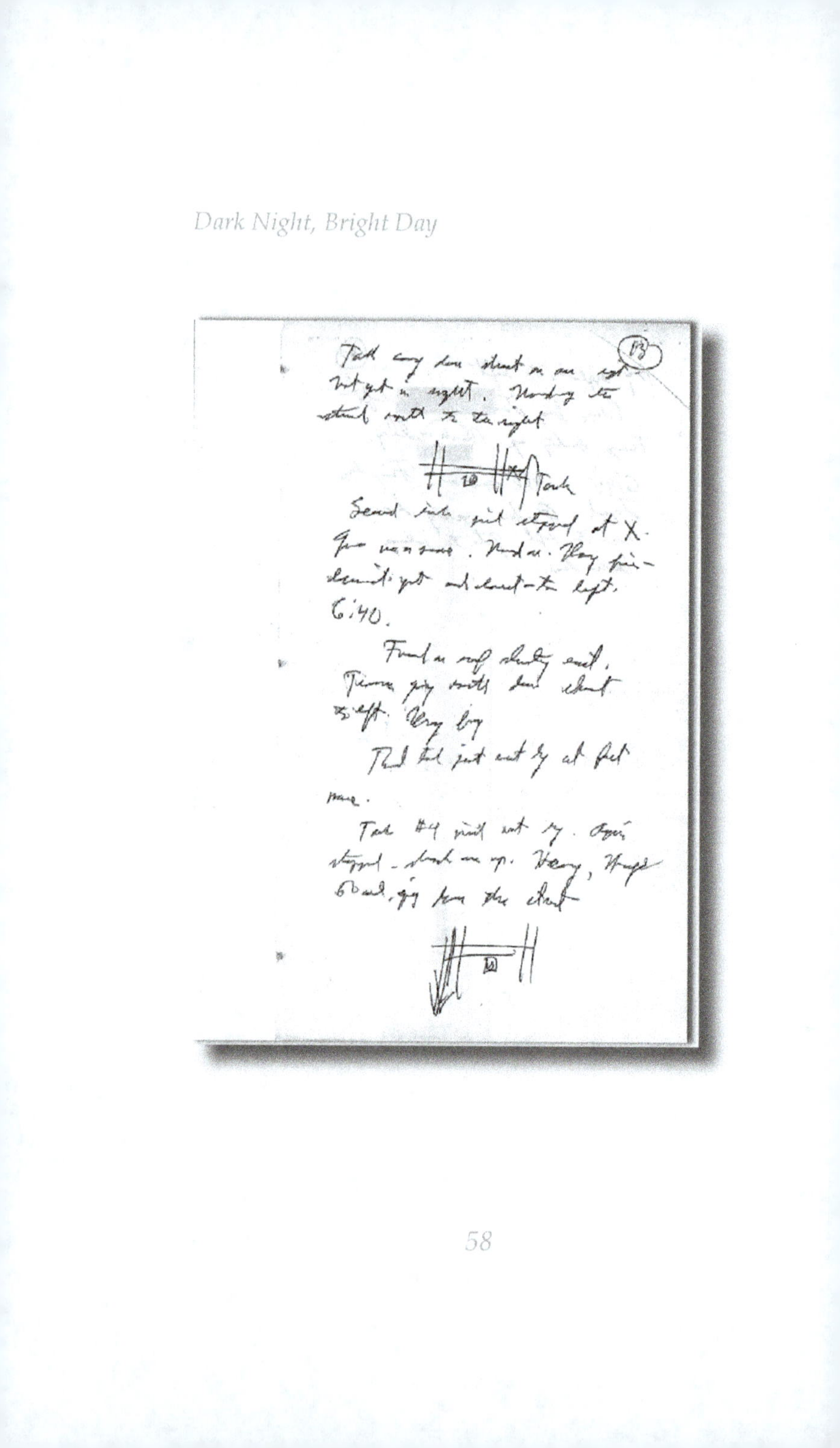

firing appearing to left

I drove firing stream to our left

Troops bolting up. Much yelling.

6.45 — All seems over. Firing has
stopped. Continue yelling here
and to left. gate to palace
broken down.

End Dark Night Bright Day

http://www.livingpresence.com/
http://bluelogic.us/